DON'T BE HORRID, HENRY!

DON'T BE HORRID, HENRY!

Francesca Simon
Illustrated by Tony Ross

Orion
Children's Books

First published in Great Britain in 2008
by Orion Children's Books
a division of the Orion Publishing Group Ltd
Orion House
5 Upper Saint Martin's Lane
London WC2H 9EA
An Hachette UK Company

A catalogue record for this book is
available from the British Library.

Printed and bound in China

www.orionbooks.co.uk
www.horridhenry.co.uk

For Judith Elliott . . .
probably the world's best editor

CHAPTER 1

Henry was a horrid baby.

He screamed in the morning.

He screamed in the evening.

At night he never slept.

He put breakfast
on his head . . .

. . . lunch on the floor

. . . dinner on the walls.

And his nappies . . .

what

a

stink!

Then Peter was born.

CHAPTER 2

Peter was a perfect baby. He smiled
all day and slept all night.

His nappies were never dirty

(well, almost never).

Henry was not very happy when
Peter arrived. In fact, he was furious.

"I've had just about enough of this
baby," he said to Mum.

"Gootchie gootchie goo," said Mum.

"Time to take that baby back to the hospital," he said to Dad.

Who's my little plumpikins?

said Dad.

Henry glared at Peter.
This house isn't big enough for
both of us, he thought.

CHAPTER 3

Horrid Henry tried posting Peter.

He tried dumping Peter.

He tried losing Peter.

He tried letting the wind
blow him away.

Perhaps he'll leave,
thought Horrid Henry hopefully.

Unfortunately, Peter didn't.

He just grew bigger and bigger,
sitting in Henry's chair . . .

27

playing with Henry's toys,

swinging on Henry's swing,
and being a total nuisance.

"Mum! Peter's kicking me!"
screamed Henry.

Don't be a tell-tale, Henry!

"Dad! Henry's knocking down my Lego!"

"Don't be horrid, Henry!"

"Why doesn't Peter
ever get into trouble?"
muttered Henry.

CHAPTER 4

Then Horrid Henry had a
wonderful, wicked idea.

"Peter," said Henry sweetly, "would
you like to dig a hole to China?"

"Oh yes," said Peter.

Henry pointed to Mum's
newly-dug flowerbed.

"Dig here," he said. "It's easier."

Peter started digging.
Soon there was a lovely big hole.

"That's great work, Peter,"
said Henry. "Why not show Mum?"

Peter toddled off.

Tee hee,
thought Horrid Henry.

Mum came outside.

"AARGHHH!"
she screamed.

"Henry! How dare you dig
up my flowerbed!"

"I didn't do it," said Henry.
"Peter did."

"Don't be horrid, Henry!" shouted Mum. "Go to your room!"

"It's not fair!" wailed Henry.

CHAPTER 5

Next day, he tried again.

"Let's surprise Mum and draw her
a picture," said Henry.
"How about a Viking ship?"

"Yeah!" said Peter.

"We need a huge space," said Henry.
"I know! Let's draw on the wall!"

"On the wall?" said Peter.

"We couldn't fit a whole Viking ship on a tiny piece of paper," said Henry. "And just think how pleased Mum will be when she sees it."

"Okay," said Peter.

Henry giggled and sneaked off.
This time *he'd* get Mum himself.

"Mum, Mum, Peter's doing something
terrible!" said Horrid Henry.
"He's drawing on the walls!"

Mum ran upstairs.

"I didn't do it, my hand did," said
Peter. "It was Henry's idea."
"No it wasn't!"

"Don't be horrid, Henry!"
shouted Mum.

"But I didn't do anything!!"
said Henry.

"You're the eldest! You should
have stopped him," said Mum.

"Go to your room!"

CHAPTER 6

The next day Mum took Henry and Peter to the park. Henry felt very sad. He couldn't get rid of Peter, and he couldn't get Peter into trouble.

Maybe he could push Peter into a
puddle when Mum wasn't looking.

Suddenly a huge dog ran up to Peter.

"GRRRRRRRR!" snarled the dog.

"Help!" squeaked Peter.

Henry didn't stop to think. "GO AWAY, DOG!" he howled in his most horrid voice.

Peter started screaming.
Mum ran up.

"Don't be horrid, Henry!"

she shouted.

"Henry's not horrid," said Peter.
"He saved me."

"My hero!" said Mum.

Henry allowed his mother to hug
and kiss him. He supposed he was
happy to be a hero for a day.

But tomorrow
– *watch out!*

HORRID HENRY BOOKS